Title: Bound by the Will
Subtitle: Billionaire Romance Story
Author: Daniel Gordon

Copyright Page

From the Publisher:
Thank you for purchasing this book.

Table of Contents

Bound by the Will
Description

Ethan Smith is a well-known billionaire and womanizer. He doesn't believe in marriage since his mom abandoned him and his dad after he was born.

His only weakness is Jane who he sees as a sister. But, what happens when he is forced to marry Jane, his childhood best-friend. Will he still see her as a sister or as his wife?

Janelle Payne is a prominent lawyer at her father's firm. She has been in love with Ethan for years but knew he would never see her that way. Her first boyfriend ends up cheating on her, making her look pathetic. If she marries Ethan, will she fall harder for him or keep her feelings in check?

Chapter 1

Janelle clutched the pillow to her chest staring out into the darkness of her bedroom as tears rolled down her cheeks. The memories of that evening, a few hours ago played out in her mind over and over again.

***

She pulled up outside of Mike's apartment and got out of the car with a bag full of presents. She had bought him the Gucci Pour Homme fragrance, a gold Rolex wrist watch and Apple Air pods with changing case. She knew he would be pleased with the presents since he had been practically begging her for months to get them.

She knocked on the door and got no response. She knocked again still no response. She quickly checked the gift bag for her purse and fished out the spare key he had given her for emergency purposes. After a few seconds, she got the door unlocked and walked inside only to meet the house dark with no lights on. She switched on the light and sighed.

"I'm sure he's at home. I saw his car parked in the garage," she said to herself as she turned right and walked toward his bedroom.

She brought her hand up to knock on the bedroom door when she heard some muffled noises.

"Surprise! Happy Anniversa..." she began as she opened thc door but paused at the scene in front of her. She closed her eyes and opened them hoping that it was just a dream.

Mike who was naked and covered up to his waist by the bedspread lay atop his co-worker, Carly. Their clothes were carelessly scattered across the room as they stared at her, the intruder.

Tense silence filled the room before Carly started to giggle.

"Finally! She knows. I was starting to wonder how long it would take for you to put two and two together."

"Shut up Carly," Mike warned as he rolled off her and sighed.

"Jane, I can explain. It's not what you think it..."

Before he could finish, she had already dashed out of the room dropping the gift bag in the process. She rushed to her car, got in and placed her head on the steering.

She felt like she was suffocating and struggling to breath with all the thoughts and questions circling her brain.

"Why am I so stupid," she asked herself repeatedly.

There was a slight knock on her window bringing her back to reality.

She looked up to see Mike standing beside her car.

"Jane, I'm sorry," he sighed as he ran his hands through his hair out of frustration, "You shouldn't have seen that."

She let out a laugh devoid of humor and rolled down the window.

"How long has this been going on?" she asked the question that had been on her mind since Carly talked earlier.

He remained silent avoiding her intense gaze. Before she could ask any further questions, Carly, now dressed in his shirt, walked up to them.

"Oh! You are still here," she giggled once again earning a glare from Mike.

"Well if you must know he didn't cheat on you. He cheated on me with you. We've been together for two years before you came into the picture. Don't ask why I allowed it. We needed your money that's all."

Jane couldn't believe her ears and turned to look at Mike for an explanation but he was looking anywhere but at her.

"He's not going to deny the truth." "Besides that, you were really stupid to think that a hot guy like Mike would be interested in a nerd like you."

***

She felt stupid, used and betrayed. She had seen the signs but she had ignored them thinking she was being paranoid, Now she wished she had paid more attention to her suspicions.

She sniffled quietly and picked up her phone, calling the one person she needed at the moment, her best friend, Ethan.

She felt her heart quicken when he picked up the phone after a few rings.

"'Hello, Jane?" he grumbled sleepily.

She felt like crying out on hearing his voice.

"Jane? Are you there?" he sounded worried.

She sniffled quietly, "Yes."

"Are you okay?"

"*Why did I call him? Why?*" she thought to herself.

"Jane? I'm coming over," he simply said catching her by surprise.

"No! Y-You don't have to," her voice wavered.

"Now I'm definitely coming over!" he hung up giving her no room to protest.

She slapped her forehead with her right hand feeling stupid for disturbing his sleep.

Fifteen minutes later, she heard the sound of a key being placed into the lock and the click of the lock opening.

The door opened and she heard a nervous voice call her name as he closed the door.

"Jane?"

Ethan looked around the living room for any sign of Jane. Seeing that she was not there, he rushed to her bedroom and knocked.

"It's Ethan. Can I come in?" he asked.

"Yes," she croaked. He cautiously entered and switched on the light before taking a few steps and stopping in front of her.

"Fuck, are you okay?" he asked on noticing her puffy eyes. He kicked off his shoes and climbed onto her bed in panic.

"I caught him cheating," she responded as her vision blurred with her tears.

He leaned against the headboard and pulled her to his chest while she wept against his shoulder, his arms around her as he held her close. To say he was furious was an understatement. Jane never cried but that bastard was making the tough Jane cry.

"It was our six month's anniversary and I wanted to surprise him but..." she paused "To think I almost gave myself to him."

She sounded so fragile and vulnerable, a side of Jane he had rarely seen despite being her best-friend for over twenty years. She had always put on a brave face even when her dad kept on blaming her for her mother's death. She hardly ever cried even when her dad refused to be affectionate to her. She didn't even cry when he didn't show up for her graduation.

So for him to receive a call from her at three in the morning, he knew something was wrong and it was confirmed when he heard her voice break as if she was about to cry. He didn't even think twice to drop the project he was working on and drive down to see her.

He started to stroke her hair gently with his fingertips in a bid to calm her down.

"I'm sorry. I shouldn't have disturbed your sleep," dhe apologized still feeling guilty for calling him when he should be sleeping.

"Oh! Please don't say that. I wasn't even sleeping. Besides, nothing is more important to me than you."

"Why would he do this to me, why?" she asked with a cracked voice causing his heart to ache.

He hugged her tighter and leaned his own cheek down onto the top of her head. He then began to sway with her side to side like she was a baby.

"'Because he's a jerk and a bastard. He doesn't deserve your tears."

"I feel so stupid."

"Don't be," he said, a frown on his face.

She pulled out of the hug looking anywhere else but at him.

"No, you don't understand. I was so desperate for someone to love me that I did everything for him. I turned a blind eye to the red flags thinking that I've finally found someone who loved me. But once again I was wrong. Am I that hard to love?"

He looked down at her and wondered how horrible of a friend he was not to notice her pain. He always thought she was fine but even the strong ones could break.

He had been so busy avoiding her because of that stupid will his dad made that he had turned a blind eye to Mike. He usually did a background check behind her back on all the guys who were interested in her. This one time he failed to protect her.

Mike had just messed with the wrong girl and he was going to deal with that fool in time. Right now though, all he wanted to do was stop her tears.

He cupped her face causing her to look up to meet his sad ocean blue eyes.

"Jane, don't you ever say that again. You are the most lovable person I know. Look around you. You have so many people who love you including me. Don't you ever forget all that because of a jerk."

They stared at each other for what felt like eternity.

"Thank you, Ethan," she mumbled quietly, her voice still hoarse from all the crying. She wiped her tears while he gave her a comforting smile.

"Anything for you, Jane."

He cupped her cheek again and for a split second she forgot how to breathe or the reason why she was crying in the first place.

"it's time for you to sleep," he whispered causing her heart to race at their proximity. She nodded in agreement suddenly tired from all the crying.

He made to get up but she held his hand keeping him in place while he shot her a questioning look. "Can you stay, please?" she asked shyly while he looked uncertain.

"Are you sure? I could just go sleep in the guest room."

"No I want you to stay with me. I don't want to be alone." Her eyes were pleading for him to say yes while he chuckled.

"Okay, scoot over," He stood up and turned off the light.

She felt the bed dip slightly as he climbed back into the bed and laid down facing up the ceiling.

"'Are you just going to watch me or lay down?" he asked sarcastically as he could feel her stares burning holes into him.

She smiled and laid down, resting her head on his chest while he wrapped his hands around her waist, holding her close to himself.

"Good night, Jane." he whispered.

"Good night, Ethan," she replied with a small smile and closed her eyes. It didn't take long for her to fall asleep as the crying had drained all her energy.

Chapter 2

The sound coming from the alarm slowly brought Jane back to reality. Still feeling drowsy, she reached behind her and hit snooze on the alarm before falling asleep.

After five minutes, the alarm sounded again making Jane groan loudly as she opened her eyes. She sat up slowly, feeling the hunger pangs in her tummy. She had failed to eat yesterday since she found out about her boyfriend cheating on her.

She glanced at the alarm clock and it read past seven and quickly climbed out of bed since she had to be at work at nine that morning. She rushed to the bathroom and brushed her teeth.

As she was washing her face, she looked at the mirror and blinked several times to make sure that she was staring at herself. Her brunette hair which she had kept in a loose bun was disheveled as if it had not been combed in days. Her hazel eyes were puffy with dark-purple circles under them.

"I look horrible," she muttered to herself.

Feeling downcast and hungry, she left the bathroom and took her glasses from the bedside table, wearing them in order to aid her vision.

She climbed down the stairs, making her way to the kitchen but stopped mid-way when she heard some movements. She furrowed her eyebrows trying to figure out who could be in her kitchen.

"Did Ethan leave my door open and someone broke in?" she thought to herself but shook the thoughts away, remembering that she lived in a heavily secured neighborhood.

Taking a deep breath, she pushed the kitchen door open and gasped in surprise on spotting Ethan washing her dishes.

The sound of the door opening pulled Ethan away from his deep thoughts. He turned to see Jane standing by the door, staring at him in surprise.

He placed the cup he was washing in the sink and took few steps toward her, his eyebrows furrowed in worry. "How are you feeling?"

She suddenly felt self-conscious in her leopard print pajamas under his intense gaze. It didn't help matters that she was already looking horrible.

"I'm feeling better now. I wasn't expecting that you would still be here."

He gave her a soft smile. "I left around six this morning for a change of clothes and came back."

She smiled for the first time that morning. He hadn't abandoned her even though he had a lot to do.

"Thank you," she whispered loud enough for him to hear, looking anywhere but at him. "I'm sorry I had to burden you with my problems."

"Jane',' he called gently and softly gripped her jaw to make her look at him, "you are not a burden to me. You are my best friend and I would do anything to make you happy. Anything!"

She felt her cheeks getting hotter under his intense gaze and forced a small smile wondering if he could hear the rapid beating of her heart. He stepped back a little bit and she exhaled in gratitude.

"I know you would have done the same for me." He grinned at her before turning toward the sink.

"I can't believe you are doing the dishes. Your employees would pay a fortune to see this," she chuckled as she folded her arms while watching him in amusement.

He turned back to her still grinning, "Like I said, I would do anything for you except cook because we both know I'm a terrible cook."

She laughed out loud earning a warm smile from him. He was satisfied that she was actually feeling better instead of crying over an idiot but he still wanted to make sure that she was fine.

"Are you really fine, Jane?" he asked as he narrowed his eyes at her.

The question caught her off guard that she stopped laughing. Truly, she wasn't sure how she felt but one thing she was sure of was that having Ethan there always made her feel better.

"I don't know,"' she answered truthfully meeting his sad gaze.

"I'm not as sad as I was yesterday or maybe I'm just used to getting rejected."

"Those guys are idiots."

"No, I keep on getting heart broken. So, it's obvious the problem is me. Nobody wants a nerd who dresses up like a grandma."

Anger flashed in his eyes at her statement. "Who said that to you?" he asked as gently as he could trying to control his temper.

She remained silent wishing that she had kept her mouth shut in the first place. Ethan had always been protective of her, if not over-protective. But she knew she was right this time. She was obviously the problem.

She was the nerd who always got bullied until Ethan saved her and they became friends. They had been friends since the age of ten and Ethan had always been the popular one while she was the nerd who was lucky to have him as a friend. Nobody wanted to be her friend. The girls only befriended her because of Ethan. As soon as they got his attention, they ditched her. No one even asked her out to prom. She was that pathetic but covered it up with indifference when she was actually hurting inside.

Finally, she got to meet Mike, the only guy who ever showed interest in her. Unfortunately, he was just like the rest of them.

“Was it Mike?” he asked trying to find out if the jerk was responsible.

“No, it’s me.”

“That’s bullshit and you know that, Jane. You shouldn’t let their words get to you.”

She frowned suddenly offended. He would never understand her point of view. He had everything. Everyone loved him. He got away with everything while she had to work twice as hard as he did to be recognized.

“You don’t understand.”

“’Rhen make me understand.”

“You have girls at your beck and call ready to do whatever you want them to do. I don’t even have that. Not that I want that but I just want to be loved. Is that too much to ask? I didn’t even get asked to the prom.”

He looked pained at her words. His lips set into a tight frown as he looked directly at her, “’About prom, nobody asked you to prom because they thought you were going with me.”

"What?" she asked wanting to make sure she heard him right.

"The guys thought that you were going with me. I was also surprised when I turned up at school with Melissa and everyone was asking about you."

She stared at him in disbelief, ""How? I mean was that why you left prom early to hang out with me?"

He nodded his head and put his hands in his pants pocket. He remembered that day like it was yesterday. Jane had told him that she wasn't interested in prom. Looking back now he realized she had said that so he wouldn't feel bad for her.

He had gone with Melissa, the class president who was his latest fling when people started asking him where Jane was. It was then he knew he had failed as a friend and rushed home to spend time with her watching reruns of old shows.

"And all these time I thought nobody liked me in that way," she mumbled close to tears.

He bit the inside of his lips suddenly feeling terrible. What he never disclosed to her was that he was the reason no guy had the courage to approach her in high school and college. Nobody wanted to go against the son of a multi-billionaire who owned the school. He made sure of that just because he was afraid that she would get hurt. He couldn't bear to see her heart broken.

He had been so occupied with finding a solution to his father's will that he forgot to find out more about Mike. He could have saved her but he failed to.

She forced a smile, "I have to go to work." She turned to leave but stopped in her tracks when he asked her a question.

"Are you mad at me?" he asked worried that she was pissed that he hid it from her.

She turned to look at him with an earnest expression, "I "don't care about what happened in the past. I'm just late for work and I'm sure you are too," dhe pointed out. She frowned on noticing his choice of clothes. He was dressed in a white shirt and denim jeans, the total opposite of his usual business suit.

"Why are you not dressed for work?"

"Well...I gave myself the day off and I already told your fad that you won't be reporting to work."

"And he agreed?" she asked.

"Your dad never says no to me."

He was right. Her dad adored Ethan. He was like the son he wished she was.

"But..." she protested knowing fully well that her Dad wouldn't like that.

"We're going to binge watch that Bridgerton series that you've always wanted to watch and I'm not taking no for an answer."

Her heart warmed at his kindness. She knew Ethan enough to know that he never took a break from work. He was obsessed with it and never mixed business with pleasure. So for him to cancel all that just to be with her, made her face flush and her heart swell with happiness at his kind gesture.

"Fine. I will just go take a shower."

She rushed upstairs to her room and had a quick shower.

Stepping out of the shower, she put on a black top on gray joggers and combed her hair, putting it in a neat bun.

Looking into the mirror and satisfied with her appearance, she jogged downstairs excited to spend the day with Ethan.

She found him seated on the sofa a pizza box on his laps. He must have noticed her questioning look

"I ordered pizza."

She nodded while he patted the space next to him for her to sit.

They spent the next hour discussing the movie and fighting over the last piece of pizza like they always do.

He used the remote to reduce the volume and looked down at the sleeping beauty whose head was resting on his shoulder. She had dozed off in the middle of the movie.

She stirred from sleep and opened her eyes only to meet his.

"Marry me, Jane." he whispered loud enough for her to hear.

She blinked several times before sitting up and staring at him "What did you say?"

"I asked you to marry me."

Her eyes widened in surprise. She hadn't been dreaming after all. She burst out laughing but stopped when he didn't join in.

"You are joking, right?"

"I'm serious." He maintained eye contact staring at her seriously.

She frowned confused.

I must be dreaming. It can't be true but he looks so serious, she thought to herself.

Seeing the conflicted look on her face, he placed his hand on hers.

"I know you're confused but I think it's the best solution to our problems. You need to be noticed and respected and you can get that by being my wife."

She released her hand from his "I don't...what are you talking about?"

"Remember I told you my dad's will stated that I would only be able to inherit his properties if I get married."

She nodded. She knew that he had disclosed that to her before. She just didn't understand what it had to do with her.

He rubbed the back of his neck "He actually named the woman he wanted me to marry and it's you."

She stared at him in disbelief waiting for him to burst out in laughter and tell her it was all a joke but he was staring at her seriously.

"It's you, Jane. He wants me to marry you"

"Why? Why me?"

"Exactly, he knows that I see you as the little sister I never had. Imagine my surprise when the news came out."

"Why are you just telling me this now?"

"You were in a relationship. I didn't want to disrupt your happiness."

"I can't believe this. Why me?"

He sighed. "Thinking about it now, my dad made the right choice. I'm sure he knew I was just going to pay a random girl to be my wife."

"This is too much."

He turned to her, holding her two hands in his while staring at her intensely. "Look at the bright side, when you get married to me no one is going to disrespect you."

"What are people going to think. Nobody would believe this."

"Everyone I know wants us together no matter how ridiculous it is."

"Still," she protested.

"Jane, it's all up to you."

"But I thought you said you've found a way out."

"I only said that because I didn't want to worry you."

"Am I the only one who knows about this?" she asked.

He shook his head.

"Ryan and your dad knows but they didn't tell you because I told them not to."

She stood up and started pacing trying to process the information.

"We're just going to stay married for a year and six months to make it believable," he said trying to make her see reason. He wasn't planning on breaking the news to her that way especially when she was still upset with catching Mike cheating on her. It just kind of came out and he couldn't stop himself.

She stopped pacing and looked down at him. "That doesn't help matters. I don't want to be a divorcee especially after one year of marriage. I'm already called so many awful names, I don't want to add another."

He stood up and placed his hands on her shoulder. "Jane, you have a lot to gain than lose in this. Everyone would have no choice but to respect you and that your foolish ex would realize what a fool he was to let you go."

She turned away from him while he sighed and brushed his hair back.

"Jane, I don't believe in marriage. At the same time I don't want this but my hands are tied. I'm about to lose the company I worked so hard to revive just because my dad doesn't want me to be alone in this world."

He paused trying to calm down and then continued, “If I had a choice you wouldn’t even know about this. Whatever your decision is, I will respect it.”

She still didn’t turn to look at him, her arms folded as she tried to make sense of the situation.

“I hate myself for putting you in this uncomfortable situation so I’m just going to leave,” he stated and picked up his phone and walked out leaving her to her thoughts.

Chapter 3

To say Ethan was nervous was an understatement. He was freaking out and trying really hard not to pace back and forth because of the press. There were a few of them which he had approved to cover the wedding.

He took a glance at his wrist watch for the hundredth time that morning and cursed.

Ryan who had been watching amusedly at his friend placed a hand on his shoulder to calm him down. " It's only been five minutes, she'll be her soon," he assured Ethan.

"What if, she changed her mind at the last minute?" he voiced out his concern.

Ryan rolled his eyes. "You know more than anyone that Jane would never disappoint you."

Ethan nodded. He knew Ryan was right. Jane would never do anything to hurt him and he loved her for that. It was two weeks after he told her about the will that she agreed to marry him and he didn't waste any time in preparing for the wedding. Since he only had five months left to fulfil his father's wishes.

His thoughts were cut short when the press turned their camera to the entrance. Mr. Payne came in with Jane holding on to his arm. Ethan felt his mouth go dry on seeing her dress. It was a white silk V-neck jumpsuit which hugged her body just right, showcasing her hourglass shape. Her makeup was simple save for a nude lipstick which made her luscious lips stand out more. She looked amazing. He didn't know how long he had been staring at her until Ryan nudged him with a knowing look.

He cleared his throat and fixed his black suit. Mr. Payne acknowledged him with a nod while he handed over Jane to him.

"Hi," he greeted her as he led her to the front stage. She smiled back not meeting his eye making him more nervous.

"Did I do something wrong?" he asked.

Before Jane could offer an explanation, the judge had already started with the introduction but that didn't stop Ethan from staring at her.

Her dad had been nice to her that day. Telling her how proud he was that she was marrying Ethan. She wondered why he even kept quiet about the will when he was the lawyer who made it and clearly wanted her to end up with Ethan.

"Do you, Janelle Payne, take Ethan Smith as your lawfully wedded husband to have and to hold from this day forward, for better, for worse, for richer, for poorer, in sickness and in health until death do us part?"

She could feel everyone's eyes on her but she couldn't bring herself to say anything. She met Ethan's confused gaze and almost felt like crying.

"Why am I doing this again?" she asked herself. She was too young to get married after all she was only twenty-seven.

She knew she was about to sign a year and six months of her life to Ethan, the man she had loved for sixteen years and that scared her to the brim. She didn't know whether she could survive being with him without hoping and getting hurt at the same time because he would never see her that way.

However, she remembered the promise she had made to his father on his sick bed that she would take care of Ethan. Back then he had insisted that she would understand in time. Even though she still didn't understand his motive, she would not dare break the promise and her friend's trust in the process. So she gathered all her wit and faced the wedding officiate.

"Yes, I do."

The wedding officiate sighed in relief and turned to look at Ethan who still seemed to be shaken by the suspense.

"Do you Ethan Smith , take Janelle Payne as your lawfully wedded wife to have and to hold from this day forward, for better, for worse, for richer, for poorer, in sickness and in health until death do us part?"

"I do." He wasted no time answering wanting to get it over and done with.

They were told to exchange rings which they did while Jane was still avoiding his gaze making him worried.

"By the power vested in me, I now pronounce you husband and wife. You may now kiss the bride." the wedding officiate announced with a smile.

They both froze with Jane finally looking up to meet Ethan's shocked gaze. They hadn't discussed this. In fact they didn't plan on doing that.

He came closer, his eyes burning holes into her making her nervous. He lifted her chin and snaked his arms around her waist pulling her close.

She gasped at their closeness, her heart beating frantically against her chest as she wondered what his next move would be.

"Trust me," he whispered and leaned in. They were only inches away from each other's face when his eyes flicked down to her lips and he swallowed nervously.

He planted his lips against hers and she froze, heat spreading across her body like a wildfire. Her lips were soft and felt like home. Before he could control himself, he sucked on her bottom lip asking for entrance. She let out a moan and he took the opportunity and explored the wet cavern of her mouth. She felt high and confused as he deepened the kiss.

The sound of clapping from the guests made them pull apart so fast it felt like a dream.

The realization of what just happened hit him as they signed their marriage license. He had planned on pecking her lips but ended up doing the exact opposite. He couldn't even look at her without feeling guilty for breaking her trust. It certainly didn't help matters that he wanted to do it again.

If no one was there, he would have continued kissing her so much that he feared he wouldn't have been able to stop himself. He felt disgusted thinking about her like that when she was clearly uncomfortable.

He was still thinking of how he could escape the uncomfortable situation when the press bombarded him with questions and congratulations making him feel thankful for the distraction.

"How was it?" Ryan teasingly asked a flustered Jane who had been looking at her feet since the kiss.

"How was what?" She glared at him despite her flustered state while he raised his arms in surrender.

"The kiss, what else would I be talking about?" Ryan rolled his eyes convinced that she was playing ignorant on purpose.

She didn't have an answer for that. She truly was still trying to recover from the shock of having her best friend kiss her.

"You know I really wasn't expecting you guys to make out in front of the press," Ryan stated.

She sighed and nodded, "I wasn't expecting it either."

They hadn't drawn up a contract yet because Ethan was in a hurry to get them married as soon as possible. However, they had agreed that there would be no physical intimacy between them which had now been broken by Ethan.

Ethan found himself staring at Jane from across the room trying to gauge her reaction. If he wasn't her best-friend, he would think that she was perfectly ok but he knew her enough to know that she was asking herself a lot of questions. He decided that he just couldn't avoid her all day without making things awkward.

He finally excused himself from the press and made his way toward her and Ryan. He signaled to Ryan to give them some privacy, unbeknownst to Jane who was looking at her feet.

Scenting Ethan's cologne, she looked up to meet his piercing ocean eyes.

"Janelle, I'm sorry about the kiss. I shouldn't have done that but I didn't have a choice because of the media being present."

She felt her heart break at his words but forced a smile "You don't have to apologize. I already prepared for this," she lied.

Ethan had kissed her for the press. This was going to be on the news the next day which would make their marriage more believable. That was why he did it and not for any other reason. She felt stupid thinking that maybe it meant something to him when it clearly didn't.

"I already made sure that the press wouldn't bother you and answered questions on your behalf."

He scanned the registry for a few seconds before turning his attention back to her "It's time to go home so just smile and hold on to my arm as I lead you outside to the car."

She nodded and obeyed with the cameras zooming in on them as they left the registry.

She exhaled in relief on entering the car after feeling overwhelmed with the cameras.

"Are you okay?" Ethan asked in concern.

She was startled out of her thoughts by his question and looked up only to see him leaning toward her. Her eyes widened at the proximity and blushed hard as she suddenly remembered the kiss they shared a few minutes ago.

She nodded and shifted putting a little space between them on the pretense of adjusting her dress so that he wouldn't be suspicious.

He narrowed his eyes at her not buying for a second that she was okay but decided to let it go. He turned to face the road and starting the car and drove away.

The silence in the car was suffocating him and he couldn't help but think that he was at fault for making things awkward between them by kissing her. He cleared his throat gaining her attention.

"I didn't allow Bill to drive because I wanted us to have some privacy." He started taking a quick glance at her before focusing on the road as he drove.

"Privacy for what?" she asked confused, her eyes on him.

He gave her the file he had taken from his seat when he first entered the car.

"For the contract I kept on postponing due to me adding and re-adding some clauses."

She pulled out the papers and started reading through while he placed his free hand on hers stopping her from reading, his eyes still focused on the road as he drove.

"You don't have to read that now. It's just for formality sake. I just wrote what we agreed upon. We could have affairs as long as they sign an NDA and we would make appearances together when necessary. The only physical touching allowed is hugging..."

He paused and chuckled nervously, "I already broke that one."

"I'll have to draw up another contract because what happened today made me realize that maybe us kissing wouldn't be so bad."

Jane felt her heart take a crazy leap as she frowned trying to make sense of his words.

He must be joking, she thought but there was nothing on his face which gave that away.

She cleared her throat and asked, "What made you come to that conclusion?"

"I just realized that we didn't think this through. Nobody is going to believe that this is a real marriage if all we do is hug each other like we usually do as best friends. It would make things more believable if we shared a kiss when necessary."

His hand gripped the steering wheel unconsciously, as he couldn't believe that he was making that suggestion to his best friend. However, he couldn't help it. He wanted to feel those soft lips on his again and how high he felt when he kissed them. He would do anything just to taste those luscious lips of hers again just to get those feelings back.

She laughed out loud trying to hide how giddy she felt. "You are joking, right?"

"Does it look like I am?"

She gasped and looked at him in surprise wondering if she was dreaming. He had just apologized to her a while ago as if he was repulsed by the fact that they kissed and now the guy who happened to be her best friend in the whole world and who was way out of her league was asking for a kiss.

"Here we are," he announced as he pulled the car to a stop in front of the magnificent gate of his mansion. The gate opened and he drove in and parked in the garage.

She slowly got of the car and closed the door behind her.

" Are you not coming inside?" she asked in concern when she saw that he made no move to come out of the car.

"Yeah, I have some work to do at the office. I'll be back before ten o'clock tonight," he lied. He just needed some time alone to understand why he wanted to kiss her again.

He attributed it to the fact that he needed to get laid which was why he was having these weird feelings and in order not to jeopardize their friendship, he needed to leave as soon as possible before he compromised her or did something that she wouldn't be able to forgive him for.

That night she waited for him but he didn't come home and the night after that.

Chapter 4

"What about this?" Jane asked as she stood in front of Ryan displaying the black gown she wore. She was at Ryan's house trying on the clothes she had bought from the boutique.

Ryan looked up in time and frowned "Oh! God. it's a no."

"This is the third time you rejected what I picked," Jane said annoyed that Ryan had always found something wrong with her dress choices.

"Yeah that's because, I don't see any difference. You need dresses Jane not black mourning gowns.

She sighed and sat next to him on the bed. She was already exhausted. Ryan had called her a few hours ago to inform her that she and Ethan were going to a business dinner.

To say she was amazed was an understatement. Ethan hadn't bothered to call her, neither had she seen him for two weeks since their wedding. It was like he was avoiding her and she didn't know what she had done wrong to deserve it. Ryan was his spoke person who tried to alleviate her worry that Ethan was just busy but she knew better.

"I'm sorry okay. I was just trying to help."

"Well, you're not helping. You keep on typing on your phone instead of helping me pick dresses and when I pick one, you dislike it. Weren't you the one who said I should change my look in the first place?"

He sat up and said, "Yeah I was the one. Have you forgotten how beautiful you looked in that jumpsuit I chose for your wedding? "

"You know what, this is a bad idea." She made to stand up but he pulled her back down.

"No, it's not. You signed up for this. What would everyone think if you didn't attend this dinner with him as his wife? It would create gossip and make everyone doubt your relationship."

"Besides, everyone will be interested in you and your background which is why you have to put more efforts in your outfits."

She sighed knowing that he was telling the truth but that didn't make her feel any better.

"So I'm only needed when he needs to make an appearance and he will disappear soon after, leaving me in the dark," she stated bitterly.

He placed his hand on your shoulder, squeezing it reassuringly. "We both know this marriage is nothing but a joke to him but it means so much to you because you love him."

She looked at her hands suddenly finding interest in her fingers. Ethan had met Ryan in college and introduced him to her. Since then they had been as thick as thieves. He knew more than anyone that she had feelings for Ethan.

"You know sometimes I stare at him and I'm amazed at how much of a fool not noticing you. Like, it's so disheartening but at the same time I warned you about this. Will your heart be okay doing this?"

That was a question she didn't have an answer to. She had thought about Ethan's offer of marriage over and over before accepting it. She had thought that she would be indifferent and would be able to keep her feelings in check but she was so wrong. The fact that he was avoiding her after their kiss only showed her that he would never love her that way and that broke her heart.

Seeing her faraway look and not wanting to make her sad, he decided to change the subject,

"You know what, I bought some dresses for you before you came over."

He called his help over and whispered something into her ear while Jane looked on confused.

"What are you doing."

"Just wait and see," he said as he winked at her while the help left.

The help came back a few minutes later with a rack full of gowns of different colors and lengths.

"I'm not wearing those." She shook her head as she stared at the rack in wonder.

"You are. In fact you must."

"Whydo I have to wear these?"

" You signed up for this. Just think of it as a wedding gift"

Just then Ethan walked in, dressed to the nines in his expensive dark blue suit.

"Hi guys," he greeted them with a smile.

"What's going on here and why are you looking so downcast," he asked as he stared at Jane who had a forlorn look on her face.

"Ah! Thank God you're here. Please help tell Jane that she needs to change her look."

Ethan frowned, his hands in his pocket as he looked confusedly at Ryan. "Why does she need to? She's okay the way she is."

Ryan face palmed himself and sighed. "You know how vicious the media can be. This is going down in history. We have to make an effort to make it believable."

"Fine, I will change," Jane declared and picked up a dress before heading for the bathroom to change. Anything to get away from Ethan.

"She didn't even look at me or acknowledge my presence," Ethan muttered under his breath but loud enough for Ryan to hear.

Ryan rolled his eyes at his friend's foolishness. "Yeah Duh! What kind of a man leaves his wife hanging for two weeks after their wedding? Did you really expect her to hug you after ghosting her?"

"Yeah ,you're right."

"I'm always right," Ryan maintained, "But seriously, why did you leave Jane hanging like that. She didn't deserve that. You made her think that she did something wrong. What is wrong with you, man?

How could he tell Ryan that he was running away from his confusing feelings for Jane? He had gone years seeing her as a sister and nothing else until the kiss happened and unlocked something in him.

How could he tell him that he needed some time away to process his emotions and find out why he wanted so badly to push her against the wall and kiss her senseless.

Jane stepped into the room dressed in a dark blue straps V-neck side slit floor length dress and stood in front of Ryan showcasing her dress.

Ryan eyes widened as he stared at her dress before standing up and smiling widely. "My God! This is it. It looks so good on you," he commented.

"If I weren't gay, I would never let you slip away."

"What do you think, Ethan?" Ryan asked Ethan.

Jane glanced at Ethan who seemed to be scanning her dress, his eyes held a mystery which made her anxious.

The dress hugged her curves in the right places making him light-headed. He had never wanted to bed a woman as much as he did right now. He yearned to bury himself inside her for hours and give into the pleasure he had denied himself for so long.

He had never felt this way about a woman before and the fact that he was feeling this way for Jane, his best friend, scared him more than anything.

"I don't like it. It's too revealing," he said for his own sanity. He couldn't be by her side all night in that dress. She was going to be the death of him.

Anger flashed in her eyes at his audacity. "I'm wearing this dress whether you like it or not." Even though she wasn't comfortable in the dress, she wouldn't allow Ethan to boss her around especially not after he abandoned her.

Ryan raised his eyebrow at him as if saying, "what is wrong with you?"

"Suit yourself." He buried his hands in his pocket and glared at her "Meet me downstairs when you are done." With that being said, he walked out.

Chapter 5

She hadn't said a word to him since they arrived at the party, although he should be thankful for that. Her silence was driving him crazy and it didn't help matters that all eyes were on them especially on Jane who looked absolutely beautiful.

He was trying really hard not to gawk at her in that dress.

"Look who we have here, my favorite man Ethan Philips," Ben Pratt said as he walked up to Ethan and Jane.

Ethan smiled on noticing his company's loyal customer, Ben, and they shared a quick hug while Ben eyes were focused on Jane who wanted to be anywhere but there at that moment.

"Is she ...your wife?" he turned to look at Ethan who nodded. "I mean I saw it on the news but I had a hard time believing that the chronic womanizer had gotten married."

He smiled at Jane. "But now I can see why you decided to settle down. She's such a pretty young lady."

"Hi, I'm Ben...Ben Pratt and you are?" he introduced himself as he shook her hands marveling at how soft her hands were.

"Janelle Pay...Smith." She quickly corrected herself smiling nervously.

"I must say Ethan got himself a priceless jewel."

She forced a smile not really pleased with the way he was looking at her.

Ethan cleared his throat catching Ben's attention. "What brings you here?" he asked trying to hide his annoyance.

Ben chuckled finally looking at Ethan. "Jaden Macauley is here and he wants to speak with you."

Ethan eyes lit up at the information. Jaden Macauley was the biggest billionaire America ever produced and he also happened to be his role model. He had always wanted to meet him and here he was.

"Come, I'll take you to him. You can thank me later." Ben offered while Ethan looked back at Jane, reluctant to leave her alone all to herself. However, she smiled at him encouraging him to go. He sighed and followed Ben.

It had been ten minutes since Ethan had left and she was bored. She didn't like being the center of attraction especially with the men eyeing her and the woman giving her the side eye. She wished she had listened to Ethan and just picked a dress she was comfortable in.

A woman stood a few feet away from her catching her attention. She wore a white see through lace gown which left little to the imagination. Her blonde hair was packed up in a bun, with two strings of hair falling over her face. She took a sip out of her wine glass while scanning Jane's dress with distaste.

"Ethan really disappointed me, you know."

Jane raised her eyebrow in question wondering why the gorgeous woman was talking to her.

"When he told me he had gotten married, I expected better not a low life like you."

"Excuse me?" Jane frowned surprised by the insult.

The woman threw her head back chuckling. "He told me everything about this sham of a marriage. He was with me the night of your wedding. We made sweet love and he was screaming my name all night. But don't worry I won't tell anyone."

Jane eyes widened as she took in the information. She felt like she had just been kicked in the stomach. She scanned the room for Ethan and spotted him happily chatting with Jaden Macauley.

So he couldn't even honor our wedding night, she thought sadly.

Jane had a few words for the stupid woman in front of her but she held back deciding not to give her the pleasure of knowing she got under her skin. She forced a smile and walked away looking for the waiter in need for a drink.

She was about to down her second glass of vodka when it was snatched away by Ben.

"Nah I can't let you get drunk." He downed the vodka on her behalf.

"How is that any of your business?" she snapped. Everyone seemed to be dictating how she should live her life while they had fun forbidding her to the same.

"With the way you were burning holes into Ethan from across the room, I would say he did you wrong." He gave her a knowing look.

"Í wouldn't blame you though what kind of a husband would leave his wife alone."

"Your Point?"

"My point is, you deserve better than him. He can't stay faithful to you neither can he respect you. You need a capable and loving man."

"What is going on here?" Ethan asked as he approached them. He had been engrossed in his chat with Mr. Macauley until he noticed Ben's disappearance. He didn't think twice to know that he would be flirting with Jane.

"Just keeping your wife company since you abandoned her."

"I think your work is done here, you can leave now!"

"I think we should let her decide that." Ben turned to look at Jane who rolled her eyes yearning to leave the party.

She made to leave but Ethan held her back making her glare at him "Let me go," she said as she tried to get out of his grip but he was too strong for her.

"We came together. We leave together," he said with an air of finality.

"Don't you think it would be better if you leave with one of your conquest here. Since that's what you are good at," Jane said.

He frowned confused. "What are you talking about?"

Ben chuckled. " You are really naïve."

Ethan glared at Ben who lifted his hands in surrender and walked away knowing better than to provoke him any further.

"Let me go," she said as she tried to wriggle out of his grip on her hand.

"Don't cause a scene," he warned.

"Of course, all you care about is your damn reputation."

Ethan regarded Jane for a moment before releasing her hand and following her out of the party.

"What are you talking about?" he asked. He didn't know what he had done to make her so angry.

She didn't answer him. Instead she kept on walking until she reached the car.

"Jane I'm talking to you." He was slowly losing his temper by her attitude.

She turned to look at him. "Would you like to talk here especially when everyone is looking at us."

She was right. There were guests outside having a drink or two and they were starting to stare at them.

They got into the car while Bill, his driver, drove the car.

Throughout the ride home, she was just looking outside the window ignoring him as if he wasn't there. He wanted so badly to ask her questions and put this behind them but he couldn't do it with Bill present so he just kept his mouth shut until they entered the house.

"Look Jane, I'm sorry that I left you alone. That was so cruel of me," he apologized as he closed the front door behind him.

She let out a laugh devoid of humor shaking her head at him. "You disgust me."

"What? What did I do?" he was genuinely confused.

She rolled her eyes. "Oh! Please. You know what I'm talking about. You left me hanging in the dark for two weeks. Two weeks! You didn't even call or text me. I was worried sick about you only for you to call Ryan and tell him that you were okay."

She paused taking a deep breath then continued "Then I decided to put my anger aside and follow you to that party. Guess who came to meet me?" she asked moving closer to him, her hazel eyes piercing his.

He remained silent knowing better than to interrupt her when she was venting.

"Your mistress! You told her about this marriage being a sham when we both agreed that nobody else apart from Ryan would know about this. I was worried sick all this time but you were somewhere fucking your mistress." She yelled the last part causing him to take a step back. He had never seen her, this angry, ever.

He already knew who she was referring to. It was Clara a top model one of his many flings. He had called her over that night to get laid and clear his head from his improper thoughts about Jane. However, he failed miserably because nothing happened between them to his dismay.

"Nothing happened between me and Clara okay," he clarified "I may have told her the truth when I was drunk but nothing happened."'

"I don't care!" she yelled.

"Then why are you so angry?" he yelled back.

"I'm angry because my 'so called best friend' left me hanging with no explanation at all. I deserve an explanation!"

He closed the space between them, their nose almost touching. To say that she was intimidated was an understatement, she took a step back but before she could move away any further, he held unto her free hand and pulled her toward him making her collide with his chest.

"What are you doing?" she managed to ask.

He smiled. "What I should have done a long time ago."

Before she could digest his words, he leaned in and touched his lip with hers, the second he touched her soft plump lips he lost himself to the hunger inside him and pushed his tongue past her lips to swim the depths of her mouth. A soft sigh escaped her throat before her tongue twined with his exploring his mouth as he did hers. It only takes her few seconds to realize that she was kissing her best friend whom she was supposed to be furious with. She gathered all her strength and pushed him away.

He sighed and brushed his hair back in frustration. "I want you so much it hurts and I'm not going to apologize because I'm not sorry. That's why I left because I can't keep my hands to myself when I'm with you."

Her body tingled under his sinfully dark gaze. She couldn't believe her ears. Her mind was in disarray at his confession. She should be jumping for joy because he wanted her but she just stood there more confused than ever.

He caressed her cheeks causing tingles on her body. "Tell me to stop."

Jane wasted no time in wrapping her hands on the back of his neck and capturing his lips with a searing kiss. He took over by kissing her back hungrily and before she knew it, he had reached down and lifted her up by the hips, her back resting against the wall with her legs wrapped around his waist.

She nearly whined when he broke the kiss. His eyes searched hers looking for any form of regret but he smiled when he only saw lust. He kissed her again carrying her easily as he turned and slowed down. He broke the kiss for a second to open the door and when they entered she realized they were in the guestroom.

Placing her down gently so her feet connected to the floor, they both kicked off their shoes as he walked her backward toward the bed.

Laying her down gently on the bed, he crawled between her parted legs. He connected his lips to hers more urgently this time. He gave her lower lip a gentle suck, then a nibble asking for permission which she immediately granted.

He moved to her neck mapping every inch with kisses and bites leaving his marks. He continued to trail a line of kisses under her collarbone, up her neck. By now she was a moaning mess so lost in her pleasure that she didn't notice when he stripped her clothes off leaving her completely naked before his hungry eyes.

"You are beautiful, Janelle," he whispered.

He went straight to cup her left breast, licking a strip over the most sensitive part. He sucked on it gently making her head fall back into a mass of pillows, back aching in impossible pleasure.

"Fuck!" she moaned lowly.

He gave it a hard suck before moving to the next mound repeating the same action.

He trailed kisses down her stomach making her squirm. His fingers made a shallow deep rubbing over her mound which made her eyes roll back and her entire body squirm.

She moaned loudly biting her lip to stop herself from screaming. His fingers retreated and she sighed in both relief and disappointment but it didn't last long.

Before she could control her breathing, he was down between her legs as she felt a warm breeze on her core. He began to flick his tongue sucking and circling making her yelp.

"Oh my God! Ethan," she cried out.

He began to pick up the pace, his fingers dipping in and out of her quickly. Her hand gripped his hair so hard she feared she might have ripped some of it. One second she was moaning for more, the next she was crying and begging him to stop.

She opened her eyes to meet his darkened eyes, giving off a hunger she knew her eyes also reflected. She watched him slowly unzip his trousers and with one pull, it fell to the ground in a heap. Her eyes zeroed on the bulge through his black boxers an ache spreading between her legs.

Suddenly afraid at how huge he was, she confessed, "Ethan...ï...I have never done this before."

"Not even with Mike?" he asked in disbelief.

She shook her head. To say he was shocked was an understatement. The right thing to do now was to stop this and pretend it never happened but he couldn't. It was too late, he was down too deep. No one had ever aroused him that much.

He took off his top revealing his toned stomach and pulled his boxers down.

He leaned over her on the bed and swept her mouth with his tongue. "I promise to be gentle."

She nodded bracing herself. She desperately desired him even though she was nervous.

Wasting no time, he settled between her thighs again aligning himself with her. He pushed in gently, inch by inch, to slowly allow her to adjust until he was completely seated. He then caught her whimpers with a deep kiss.

He let her breathe for a second before he slowly started to pick up pace. He leaned up on his arms thrusting into her faster and faster while her fingers wrapped around his muscular back gripping on for dear life as moans and groans filled the room.

He changed the angle by pushing her legs higher around his waist. He began to thrust even harder and quicker making her scream in pleasure, nails digging his back. "Oh, God, Ethan. Ethan...aah...aah."

His eyes locked unto hers as their bodies connected. One hand was on the back of his neck, the other under his arm, clawing at his back.

His eyes were locked unto hers, studying her every reaction.

Feeling her tighten around him, he increased his pace as he pursued his own release.

"Just let go."

As if it was the magic word, her feet curled and her body arched. Jane screamed her orgasm yelling his name.

His real undoing was watching her orgasm as he soon found release groaning her name.

Ragged moans left his parted lips as they let each other ride their pleasures until the end. With one last thrust, he stilled inside her

"Wow!" he exclaimed.

He slowly pulled out of her still sensitive body in a bid not to crush her and dropped next to her. They laid there catching their breath.

He stood up and left for the bathroom.

A few seconds later he came back with a warm towel and started to wipe the blood between her legs. It took every will power in him not to take her again. He disposed of the towel and climbed in bed with her.

She could feel herself being pulled to sleep when she felt him wrap his arms around her before pulling the covers over them.

The last thing she felt was him placing a gentle kiss on her neck before she fell into the best sleep she had ever had.

Chapter 6

Sunlight invaded the bedroom through the large windows hitting his face. He frowned and squinted his eyes to adjust to the light.

He laid there for a few seconds confused on why he was not in his room. He then became aware of the weight on his arm and the constant airy tickle at the back of his neck.

His heart skipped a bit as the memories of last night replayed in his head. He had actually had sex with Jane, his best friend.

"Shit," he grunted quietly.

As he stared at the sleeping girl next to him, his heart sank with the fact that he had taken her virginity. An honor he didn't deserve. He had had plenty of sex in his life time but they all faded in comparison to last night.

He slowly removed his arm from underneath her sleeping frame and climbed out of bed as quietly as possible.

He carefully picked up his boxers and shirt and put them on. He eyed her sleeping figure one last time before he slipped out.

He needed to get out of there as soon as possible. She deserved better than him. Last night had already established that she wanted him as much as he wanted her and although that pleased him. Those new found feelings scared him. He couldn't afford to let his demons consume her.

The thought of wanting to be with her forever, haunted him because he knew what it implied but he was not ready for that. He doubted that he would ever be.

He had commitment issues. If he had been afraid of getting hurt before, now he was afraid that he would be the one to hurt her.

He had watched how his dad pined after his mom even after she abandoned him for another man. He never recovered and that had no doubt contributed to his illness which later led to his death six months ago.

After watching his dad wallow in self-pity, he had vowed to never let a woman capture his heart. Jane had been the only constant woman in his life and now he had ruined that by being intimate with her.

He needed a cold shower. He rushed to his bathroom and stayed in the shower for ten minutes before stepping out and sighing.

Ten minutes later, he climbed down the stairs now dressed in a dark blue pressed suit.

Desperately in need of a drink, he went to the bar and brought out a bottle of whiskey. He popped it open and downed the content not bothering to pour it into a cup. He placed the bottle on the bar table and exhaled. He never drank in the morning especially when he had to be at work in a few minutes time but the events of last night called for something strong to deal with it.

His thoughts were interrupted when he heard someone approaching. He looked up in time to see Jane approaching him.

He swallowed hard as his eyes trailed down her night robe dying to feel her under him again.

She had a glint in her eye as she smiled at him. "I thought you left me alone." She had woken up a few minutes ago looking for Ethan thinking that maybe he regretted what happened between them. Now she was relieved that he didn't leave her like an insignificant one night stand.

She could feel the awkwardness in the air as Ethan nervously looked anywhere but her.

Call her naive but she needed to know where they stood. She didn't regret last night. She was happy that it was the man she loved that she slept with.

Hating the silence she cleared her throat catching his attention. "Ethan, can we talk?"

He froze and licked his lips nervously. "If this is about what happened last night, forget it."

Her heart sank "Why?"

He looked down at the bottle suddenly finding interest in its content ."Last night was a mistake. It shouldn't have happened. I'm sorry."

She felt her lungs tighten as she winced at his words.

"It didn't mean anything to you?" she said to herself but he heard her.

"Yes, it was just sex, nothing else." He felt like a jerk breaking her heart like that. He had never been cruel to a woman even his flings but the one woman he cared about, he was treating her like trash.

She could feel herself wanting to cry but she would be damned if she did so in front of him. She took a few deep breaths to keep herself calm and slapped herself mentally for being so stupid. She should have seen it coming but she had let her hopes take over and now she was paying the price.

"It meant a lot to me because I gave myself to the man I love and I don't regrct it."

He stood up from his seat "You love me?" He couldn't have heard her correctly.

She rolled her eyes at his stupidity. "I've always loved you. I was there when you moved from all the Melissas and Kims in town. I was in the side lines hoping that one day you would see me and I thought that last night meant something to you but I thought wrong."

"What the hell!" he muttered under his breath.

She had always loved him and now he had broken her heart beyond repair. To think he was initially worried that he had lost her friendship but alas, he had done worse.

He ran his fingers through his hair and bit his lips hating himself for what he was about to say next. "Is that why your dad manipulated my dad into forcing me to marry you? You just couldn't stay in the side lines any longer and took advantage of my vulnerability last night."

She slapped him hard on his cheek causing him to gasp in surprise. He knew he deserved it. He deserved worse from her.

"Fuck you, Ethan. I can't believe this is you." The tears she had been trying to prevent, rolled down her cheeks as her voice broke.

"Well you better believe it. Did you really think you could change me just because of a one night stand?" he scoffed "You are really naive."

"It was just sex. It meant nothing to me so the sooner you get over it, the better for the two of us," he snapped.

She shook her head as she stared at him with tear stricken eyes. He didn't look or sound like the man she loves. He was different. The total opposite of the caring Ethan she had always known. If she knew that sleeping with him would unleash the devil in him, she would have stopped last night from happening.

She wiped her tears and forced a smile. "Fine. It's totally fine."

She looked away and sniffed. "I'm not going to stand here and be disrespected while pretending that everything is fine. My job here is done. You've gotten your inheritance, there's no need for any more pretense."

"Don't worry, we'll stay married as stipulated in the contrac,t but I'm not going to live here anymore nor am I going to go out on dates with you pretending that we're a happy couple."

She quickly turned away headed for her room to pack her stuffs. She muttered a sorry to Ethan's father. She couldn't do this anymore. She just couldn't.

He fell down to his knee, his heart pounded against his chest as he started to tremble. He didn't mean any of what he said. He wanted so badly to beg her not to leave, to tell her that he would change for her. It hurt him to hurt her like that but he was a lost case. She couldn't fix him, no one could.

She climbed down the stairs dragging her luggage with her. She spotted him on the floor and almost rushed to ask if he was okay but she stopped herself. She couldn't be a fool anymore and run to him every time like a lap dog. He didn't need her, he never needed her.

She walked past him to the door and gave him one last look "Goodbye Ethan". and banged the door after her.

Her words were cold and distant and the finality behind them hit him hard.

"Goodbye Ethan." It kept on ringing in his ear.

"This is what you wanted so why does it feel like my heart is being ripped out off my chest." he asked himself.

He knew the answer to that. If he had been ignoring his feelings before, there was no point now. He couldn't deny it anymore. He was in love with her totally and completely.

Chapter 7

Jane pushed the strand of hair that had been disturbing her vision behind her ear as she studied the file before her. It contained the facts of the divorce case she was in charge of. The couple had cited irreconcilable differences as grounds for their divorce and it made her think of Ethan.

She hadn't seen or talked to him in two months and it was driving her crazy. She wished he would just walk in and apologize and they could go back to being friends at least but that was all wishful thinking. The mere fact that he didn't bother to contact her convinced her the more that he was done with her.

Her stomach grumbled. "I just finished eating an hour ago." She pouted and glanced at clock. It read 11am.

She had just finished eating pizza and toast and now she was craving mashed potatoes and ice-cream and it wasn't even lunch time yet.

A knock came on the door.

"Who is it?" Jane asked as she rubbed her stomach.

"It's Martha."

Jane smiled thanking God that her secretary came at the right time. "Come in."

"Ma'am, a man by the name of Ben Pratt is here to see you."

Jane frowned at the information wondering why Ben was there to see her and how he knew her office.

"Let him in and... please get me some mashed potatoes and ice-cream."

She looks surprised by Jane's request, "But ma'am I got you pizza and French toast a few hours ago."

"Yes now I want something else."

She sighed and left.

Jane knew that it hadn't gone unnoticed to her colleagues that her eating habits had changed and in the process she had gained weight. She could sometimes hear the snide remarks she got as she walked by with some of them calling her a pig. However, she wasn't going to ignore her cravings and starve herself just because of other people's opinion.

Ben entered into her office smiling.

"Finally! I get to see you again," he said as he embraced her. She wondered when they had gotten so close for him to hug her.

"I'm surprised you know where I work"

"Well I have my ways."

"Please have a sit."

He obliged and sat down in front of her.

"What brings you here?" Jane asked curiously.

"You." His answer shocks her and she give him a questioning look.

He bursts out in laughte.r "I'm just joking but it's not far from the truth."

He sat up and straightened in his seat.

"I was looking forward to seeing you on that business trip with Ethan but he was alone and you were nowhere in sight. It was then I knew there was trouble in paradise."

Her heart raced as she pondered on what to say to counter his words. Nobody was supposed to know that they were no longer together.

"He was a mess on that trip. He spent time drinking and smoking until he lost the deal. I thought he would hook up with the ladies throwing themselves at him but I was surprised when he didn't. He really has it bad for you."

"Why are you here?" she asked wondering why he was talking about Ethan when everyone knew that they were frenemies.

"Good question." He folded his arms and leaned back on the chair

"Only a few set of people know that you guys are separated. If I must tell you I was glad because I have a crush on you. But seeing him so depressed and broken, I just had to see you."

He paused for a moment as if thinking over his next words.

"I've been in your guys shoes before. I let her go because I was a coward and too afraid to face my feelings but here I am still hurting while she has a family now."

"Tell it to Ethan." She didn't want to hear about this.

"I tried but he won't listen to me."

"Well, I'm the wrong person to talk to," she snapped.

"He pushed me away. I can't go back to someone who doesn't love me or respect me."

She could feel a headache coming. She rubbed her forehead with her hands while Ben looked on worried.

"Are you all right?" he asked in concern.

"Yeah I'm fine. It's just a headache."

He studied your face for a moment and shook his head. "You're not fine. I can see the dark circles under your eyes. You haven't been sleeping, Janelle."

"Why are you acting, as if you know me?" she was getting pissed off now.

He raised his hands up in defense."I'm just trying to help."

She was about to tell him that he was not helping when her dad barged in, banging the door behind him.

"Dad?" she stood up in shock as she watched her fuming dad.

"Don't you dare dad me. What is this?" he asked as he showed her his phone screen.

She gave him a skeptical look before glancing at the phone and reading the content out loud

"Well known billionaire, Ethan Smith's marriage has hit the rocks in just three months. Click here for more details."

"Is this why you've been spending late nights at the office? Is Ethan already tired of you?" he asked as he withdrew his phone from her sight.

She kept quiet unable to say anything in her defense.

"I think you should just calm down and discuss this issue like normal adults," Ben suggested sensing the tension in the room.

"And who are you?"

"I'm ..." Ben was cut off by Jane's father.

"I don't give a damn about who you are but if you have any manners you will know that you shouldn't meddle in family matters."

"I can't just sit here and watch you talk to her like that!"

She couldn't stand the shouting and the arguments anymore. Her migraine was getting worse and she was starting to feel dizzy.

"Please stop," she managed to say as she blinked trying to keep herself awake.

"Are you all right?" Ben was now standing by her side holding onto her hands.

She wanted to say that she was fine, that there was nothing to worry about but the next thing she saw was black.

Ben quickly caught her before she hit the floor, carrying her immediately in a bridal style.

"Jane!" Mr. Payne yelled her name as he rushed to her side.

"Call an ambulance!" Ben yelled at Mr. Payne who looked around confused for a moment before he dashed out.

Chapter 8

"You've got to stop doing this?" Ryan said as he stared at his friend, Ethan who had just woken up after spending the night drinking. He was lying on the bed staring at the ceiling as if there was something written on it that caught his attention.

"Stop what?" Ethan asked still not taking his eyes away from the ceiling.

"This pity party. You guys had a stupid fight which can still be resolved if you act like a man and just tell her that you love her," Ryan almost yelled. He was frustrated with his friend's antics.

Ethan had become a shadow of himself since he pushed Jane away. He had abandoned his company, his friends and drowned himself in alcohol and weed just to forget her and Ryan was tired of it. He was tired of babysitting Ethan.

"You didn't want to hurt her but you ended up hurting her. Are you happy now? That woman has loved you even before she knew what love was. She has always been by your side, through your pains and tribulations. She was always there and you just had to be a coward and chase her away because you are too afraid to accept that you have fallen for her," he yelled this time not holding anything back.

This time Ethan looked at him and sat up. "Why arc you yelling at me?"

Ryan stood up from where he sat at the left side of the bed and bent down to look at Ethan. "Because I'm trying to knock some sense into you!"

"Your greatest fear has come true because you have turned into your mother!"

Ethan winced hating that he was right. Everyone was right. He was an asshole who hated his mother but he was just the same.

"I just hope it won't take too long for you to come to your senses because I won't be there to console you when she ends up with a better man!"

"Is there something you are not telling me?" Ethan asked suddenly finding interest in Ryan's outburst. He couldn't picture Jane with another man. He just couldn't.

Ryan was about to say something when his phone rang breaking the silence. He dipped his hands into his pocket and brought out his phone.

"It's Ben," Ryan said as he stared at the caller's Id.

Ethan frowned wondering why Ben would contact Ryan.

Ryan picked the call while Ethan watched as Ryan's expression changed from skeptical to worried.

"What? How is she? Yeah I'm my way." Ryan cut the call and stared at his phone for a moment.

"What happened?" Ethan asked worried. He hated being kept in the dark and something told him the news was meant for him.

Ryan looked up to meet his gaze and shook his head. "Jane fainted and was rushed to the hospital."

"what?" Ethan jumped out of bed "We have to go. Where are my car keys?" he asked as he dug into his pockets for his car keys.

"I'll drive. I can't let you drive in your state." Ryan pointed at him while Ethan looked down at himself. He knew he looked a mess but he didn't give a damn.

He rushed downstairs after Ryan who quickly grabbed his car keys from the dining table.

They dashed out of the house and entered the car. Ryan ignited the car engine and drove out of the mansion headed for the hospital.

"Will you drive faster," Ethan suggested wanting to get there as soon as possible.

"I'm trying my best, okay. Will you please stop panicking. It's not helping," Ryan said his eyes focused on the road as he drove.

"You could've just allowed me to drive."

Ryan scoffed. "Excuse me for not wanting to die before my time."

"See, we're here," Ryan declared as he pulled up to the hospital and parked his car in the parking lot.

Ethan wasted no time in getting out of the car and rushing inside the hospital. He saw a nurse behind the counter and rushed to her panting.

"Please do you know which ward Janelle Smith is admitted to? I'm her husband," he asked desperation evident in his voice.

"Hey Ethan, it's not cool that you left me out there," Ryan said as he walked in

"Can you please be fast about it?" he told the nurse who was still scanning through the register.

"Ethan?" he heard his name being called and turned to the direction of the voice only to spot Ben.

"Where is she?" Ethan asked anger laced in his voice.

"Hey, calm down."

"Calm down? What did you do to her?" He was trying to keep his cool even though it was taking every will power in him not to punch Ben.

"I didn't do anything. She fainted in her office and I brought her here."

He sighed. “Look I’ll take you there. Just follow me,” he said while they followed him into the hospital.

Mr. Payne was seated on the visitor’s seat his head on his hands when he heard footsteps approaching. He looked up in time to see the three men walking toward him with Ethan leading the way.

“Is she okay?” Ethan asked Mr. Payne in concern.

Mr. Payne sighed and shook his head. “I don’t know. We just rushed her here and the doctor hasn’t said anything yet.”

Just then the door to the room where Jane was confined opened and the doctor walked out smiling.

“How is she?” Ethan asked.

The doctor smiled at him. “You don’t have to worry about her, she’s perfectly fine.”

The doctor paused for a minute and looked between the four men. “Which one of you is her husband?” he asked.

Ethan stepped forward. “I am.”

The doctor extended his hands out for a handshake while Ethan looked on confused. “Congratulations, Your wife is pregnant.”

His eyes widened as he took several steps back suddenly losing his brain cells.

“She’s pregnant?” Mr. Payne asked rhetorically still shocked by the revelation.

“Yes she is.”

“But why did she faint?” Ryan asked.

“She fainted due to stress and lack of vitamins but there’s nothing to worry about. She just has to start her prenatal care.”

“Guy, you are a sharp shooter,” Ryan chuckled while nudging Ethan.

"Can I see her now?" Ethan asked after finding his voice. He couldn't believe he was going to be a father. It all sounded like a dream. All he wanted to do now was to bombard Jane with kisses.

"Yes you can," the doctor said. "Only one person for now."

Ethan followed the doctor inside the room.

Jane blinked several times to confirm that she was indeed seeing Ethan. He was there right in front of her, staring at her like she was some trophy that he had won.

"What is he doing here?" she asked the doctor as she pointed at Ethan.

"He said he's your husband and I just told him that you are pregnant."

She couldn't believe her ears. "I'm pregnant? This must be a joke. How is that even possible I've been seeing my period?" she asked the doctor.

"You just experienced decidual bleeding, ma'am. We've carried out the necessary tests and determined that you and your baby are in perfect health."

Jane stared at the doctor, then at Ethan who was already staring at her.

"How can I be pregnant?" she asked herself. She hadn't planned on this. It wasn't part of their plan. She scoffed. Having sex was not part of thcir plans either but they had broken all the rules in the contract.

"Jane," Ethan called as he finally gathered the courage to move closer to her.

"Don't you dare come near me," she warned. She didn't want to see him. This was too much for her to digest.

"I'm sorry. I'm really, really sorry," he pleaded as his eyes tearing up.

"No! Stay away from me. Get out!" she yelled startling him.

"Please just go." she pleaded on the brink of tears. This wasn't how she wanted her year to be. She wasn't ready to be a mother especially for a man who didn't love her.

He nodded getting the message and walked out of the room.

"Ethan, we need to talk," Mr. Payne said.

"About what?"

"You and my daughter."

Ethan crossed his arms ready to hear what Jane's father had to say.

Mr. Payne cleared his throat as he studied the young man in front of him for a second before sighing. "Before your father made his will, he called me aside and voiced his concern on how you were wasting your life away being a workaholic and a womanizer without having a woman by your side."

Ethan frowned and bit his lips. He could definitely imagine his father saying that.

"He felt guilty for being the one who made you distrustful of women. He didn't want to leave this world knowing that you would be alone so he asked me to make that will."

"Do you know why he chose Jane?" Mr. Payne asked while Ethan shook his head. He didn't know but he was dying to know.

"He couldn't find a better woman for you than Jane. She was the only woman you allowed to be close to you and he wanted that to stay forever. He didn't want you to lose her forever so he made that will."

He placed a hand on Ethan's shoulder, squeezing it reassuringly. "Don't make your dad regret making that decision."

"Why are you acting like her dad all of a sudden?" Ethan asked as he couldn't believe that Mr. Payne was actually advising him on treating Jane better; when he had spent his whole life maltreating his daughter and blaming her for her mother's death.

Mr. Payne sighed as he withdrew his hand from Ethan's shoulder. "It's never too late to repent son."

"It's never too late," Mr. Payne said as he walked away.

Epilogue

"Dad!" A five year old boy yelled as he ran across the field chasing his puppy. He slipped on the wet grass and let out a loud cry when his father rushed to him and scooped him up, swaying him from side to side.

"Don't cry, baby," he whispered while swaying his son.

"I'm not a baby," the boy said as he wiped his tears.

The man chuckled and said, "Big boys don't cry."

"I'm not crying. Something just entered my eye," the boy said while his father laughed putting his son down. The boy was so stubborn like him and it amazed him every time how the boy was too much like him. He had his blond hair and his blue eyes but he also had his mother's beauty and smile.

Speaking of his mother, a heavily pregnant woman dressed in an oversized white top and blue jeans matched with trainers walked into the field fuming.

"Ethan, how many times have I told you not to allow him to play here?" Jane asked fuming.

Ethan sighed and brushed his hair back "I'm sorry."

She frowned and crossed her arms. "That's what you said the last time."

"Jane, relax, he's just a little boy. Let him have fun."

She rolled her eyes. "He can have the fun he wants inside and not on the wet grass. I don't want him to get hurt."

"Mom I'm okay, " the boy said holding onto her leg. "You nag too much."

Her mouth opened wide in surprise as she stared between father and son. Ethan couldn't help but laugh at his son's comment.

She raised her hands up in defeat. “I don’t even know why I bother with you guys. Like father like son.” She made to leave but he hugged her from behind preventing her from leaving.

“Babe, I’m sorry.” He apologized and pecked her cheeks. He knew it was her pregnancy hormones affecting her mood.

She melted into his embrace reveling in his touch.

“I don’t know why I put up with you.” she smiled.

“Because you love me.”

They both chuckled remembering an incident from five years ago.

“Why are you here?” Jane asked Ethan who had just walked into her apartment like he owned the place while holding onto a bouquet of lilies, her favorite flower.

“To see you,” he said it like it was the most obvious thing in the world.

She had been avoiding him for a week since they both found out that she was pregnant. He simply took advantage of the opportunity that her door was open and walked in.

“Well you’ve seen me, now go.”

“Jane,” he called.

“Are you here to see the result of our one night stand or to blame me for planning this and trapping you with a baby?”

He stared at her incredulously.

“If this is about the baby, I’m keeping it. You don’t have to take responsibility as the father. I’m okay by myself.”

He groaned. “Why are you putting words in my mouth?”

“Then what else are you here for?”

He placed the bouquet on the table and said, "To apologize for being a jerk and pushing you away."

She rolled her eyes and folded her arms

"I didn't mean what I said that night. I thought I was doing the right thing by pushing you away but I ended up hurting us both."

"Is that all?"

"No Jane listen to me. I love you. I always have and it's such a pity that it took a kiss for me to realize it. That night wasn't a mistake. It meant much more to me, so much more that it scared me and I just chose the easier way out by pushing you away because I was too afraid to face my feelings."

He couldn't read her facial expression. He wasn't even sure if she was listening but he wasn't going to stop now.

"I love you, Jane. I really do but I'll understand if you don't feel the same anymore but please let me in my child's life," he pleaded.

She just stood there staring at him blankly.

"I'm sorry. I'll just go," He said as he turned to leave.

"Ethan," she called and he stopped in his tracks and turned to face her.

"I love you too." She threw herself at him while he embraced her as if he was afraid that she would slip away. They stayed like that for a few minutes until she pulled out of the hug.

"Took you two months to apologize."

"Nah, it took me two months, three weeks and two days."

She opened her mouth in surprise. "You've been counting it."

"Yeah, I couldn't help it. It's been hell without you."

"Remind me why I put up with you." she asked as she leaned her head against his.

"Because you love me," he chuckled earning a playful punch in return.

***

"Don't you think we should make another baby?" he whispered in her ear causing her to shiver.

She rolled her eyes and chuckled. "I'm already pregnant at least let me push this one out first."

"it's not too late," he said as he nuzzled her neck, taking in her fragrance.

"Mom, Dad let's go inside. I'm feeling cold," Edward said as he pouted interrupting his parent's moment.

Ethan reluctantly released Jane with a groan while the later stifled a laugh.

Edward ran inside with his mother trailing after him while Ethan stayed behind in order to catch the puppy.

He smiled at the retreating back of his son. He had named his son Edward after his father. The man who had made sure he didn't end up alone. He looked up at the sky and muttered a thank you to his dad.

His father had given him the will to love and he would never trade this all for anything.

THE END

www.ingramcontent.com/pod-product-compliance
Ingram Content Group UK Ltd.
Pitfield, Milton Keynes, MK11 3LW, UK
UKHW041643190726
13854UKWH00006B/2658